WHERE IS HELD?

HADRIAN

Also by Michael Califra:

No Man's Land
Alone.
Leaving Natalie

Michael Califra

WHERE IS HELD?

First Hadrian printing 2021

ISBN: 978-0-578-94722-8

Library of Congress Control Number: 2021914235

10 9 8 7 6 5 4 3 2 1

Where is Held?

IN THE PICTURESQUE city of Zürich, Switzerland, midway between the botanical gardens and the lake, is a modest but charming building. It houses the Swiss affiliate of the Calculated Risk Group, one of the world's largest and most powerful insurance companies.

In one big office-chic room on the second floor, the six underwriters of Calculated Risk's Property & Casualty division arrive no later than eight o'clock in the morning. They give each other perfunctory greetings, as though each is annoyed to find the other still sitting in the living rooms of their own homes. And this office was their home, or at least a second home, for they sat at tables in front of computer screens from the time they arrived until six in the evening—or seven, or eight, or sometimes later still, typing with a zealous fervor: working on and otherwise calculating 'quotes'; evaluating and interpreting statistics; emailing business offers to brokers and customers; making forecasts; engaging in planning; advising on business cases; performing portfolio analyses; calculating and estimating loss ratios; working on product development; monitoring claims; dealing with enquiries and compliance issues raised by the Swiss Financial Supervisory Office for Insurance (known as the *Finma* to all in the business), and discussing those issues with legal counsel. All this involved churning out *Excel* spreadsheets, applying pricing tools, and engaging in tedious discussions with the actuaries who had designed and developed the formulas that would then be used by the underwriters. There were also those time-consuming and regularly recurring peer reviews, which were required in addition to the day-to-day work. And of course there were the administrative chores; the *admin stuff*, as it was known: dealing with the claims department; handling accounting discrepancies; giving contracts identification numbers, and filling in the minor details of those contracts—all of which was excruciatingly tedious and also consumed vast amounts of time. All of this was done with each of the underwriters trying in any way possible to distinguish themselves from the others in the eyes of management. Mountains of work that no person could ever hope to stay ahead of unless they also worked most of the weekends from their real homes. And no one could afford to fall too far behind because if they did, catching up would eventually become impossible. Once you fell behind, the workload would grow exponentially into something really monstrous. Calculated Risk, like its competitors, and all of big business generally, had long ago gone through its period of *McKinseyization*; a process named for a firm of consultants whose job it was to save corporations big money by determining, with mathematical precision, the absolute rock-bottom number of employees needed to, at least in theory, complete the required workload. So they kept up, these employees of the Calculated Risk Group, no matter how hard or long the slog. The mere thought of failing was itself a nightmare because the world of insurance in Switzerland was a small one. Everyone knew everyone else. And everyone wanted to move up. That was the whole and entire point of it all. To attain a higher position where one earned more and had a more prestigious title. Switzerland was all about money and status. Failure on the job would be a stain on a person's record that could last for years, or if the failure was big enough, for a lifetime. So their work was expected to be the central core of their lives. Banking and insurance were the country's vital organs, and if they needed to suck the blood of its citizens to keep healthy, then so be it. In return they were paid very well, which was an absolute necessity if one resided in Switzerland, a place known for its high cost of living.

All of this, of course, required a certain character type. No one with a bureaucrat's mindset could ever function in this environment. No artistic types would ever last in this place. No *thinkers* or academics could ever hope to cut it here. One had to be a striver. A corporate ladder-climber. Only the Type-A personality could ever hope to succeed. Only the kind whose social media feed showed them living every minute of every day to the fullest: biking, mountain climbing, swimming in a frozen landscape, travelling to exotic places, surrounded by lots and lots of attractive friends. Only those who were willing to subordinate their lives to their work and be 'team players' were suited to this job. Only those who *dare take on this challenge* (as one of Calculated Risk's classified ads put it) should even consider applying for such a position.

Switzerland being a tiny nation with an oversized economy, the native-born population is not large enough to do all that needs to be done to keep the country thriving. So the underwriters of Calculated Risk's Property & Casualty division, like the rest of the company, are a mixed group: only one, Urs Gipfeli, is a native and, as he often liked to remind his coworkers, enthusiastic member of the Swiss Reserve Army. Hana duVal, the forty-year-old American who heads the group, is self-assured in her eloquence and style, but in reality is a chaotic manager. Malvina Panchevska, an attractive, curvy-blonde Pole in her early thirties sits opposite Jason Peel, late twenties, from the United Kingdom. Peel took as many nonchalant glances at Malvina as possible during the course of a day, fantasizing about what she looks like unclothed. For her part, Malvina was manipulative; with her glances, smiles, and hands on the shoulders of the men in the group, she was able to get them to take some of her workload, especially the tedious *admin stuff*. Agostina Paffuto is a chubby Italian approaching fifty, seemingly easy-going but is desperate to get ahead. And lastly, there is Gustav Held, a German, whom everyone called simply by his surname. Held is the Senior Underwriter. In his late fifties, he has been with the company for only eighteen months. Despite or because of his *Senior* title, his age, or his position as the newest member of the team, it is Held who constantly gets piles of work dumped on him by the others.

Currently it is 'renewal season,' a particularly stressful few weeks, for it is that time of the year when existing contracts expired and had to be renegotiated. Clients were expected to be persuaded to stay with Calculated Risk, and pay more for the privilege of doing so. It was a time when every underwriter had a chance to shine and to put their 'team player' encouragement toward coworkers on full display. Every renewed contract would be announced via email to everyone else, which would prompt congratulatory emailed replies such as *Bravo Italy! Bravo Poland! Let's rock!! Keep it going! Hopp Schwiiz!*

Anyone who took a look into the second-floor Property & Causality office, or any of the other offices in the building, at any hour during the long business day would notice all the underwriters typing fervently on their keyboards while staring intently at their computer screens. Yes, it happened to be renewal season, but that was not the reason for the zeal in their activity. They were always typing in that fashion; as if every piece of work, every email, every spreadsheet, every calculation, had the utmost urgency; as though the fate of the entire global company depended on what they happened to be doing at that moment. But today, their fervor was more than just intense, it was inspired, for the underwriters had just come from the conference room on the top floor where, under a horseshoe-shaped skylight they watched Calculated Risk's CEO, Mr. Alfred, live video-stream his quarterly address to all the company's employees around the world. About one hundred women and men from the Swiss office packed into the room, which was decorated in midcentury modern, and lighted by golden, torch-like sconces on the walls. Mr. Alfred said how honored he was to have "marvelous and marvelously-able" people working on his behalf. And, conversely, how those in his employ were privileged to be working for a company respected worldwide, at the very pinnacle of so necessary an industry; a company so trusted and valued that it was able to attach an extra fifteen-percent premium onto all its premiums. Without insurance, Mr. Alfred said, the global financial system itself would collapse. The lives of ordinary people would be ruined. The civilized world as we know it would cease to exist. Everything had to be insured; all risk properly assessed and premiums calculated. Policies had to be written in precise language to protect the insurer from paying one cent more than that which is absolutely necessary. "It's all about the *DOLLars*," he said in his unique accent from faraway Hartford. "Always remember that. All about the *DOLLars*." And about the dollars it was. Mr. Alfred thanked his employees for another record year of profits that had pushed the company's stock prices to the highest ever on exchanges around the world. "We will all share in the wealth you've created. I am so proud of each and every one of you." Then he recited his mantra, which had become legendary in the business world, "Remember, when you think you can't possibly work any harder, push yourself even more. That's when miracles happen." Next he answered pre-submitted, pre-screened questions from his employees in their offices in various territories, and before each, the employees in the Swiss office felt a rush of anticipation, hoping one of theirs would be next to be answered with the canned preface,

"That is an *excellent* question, I'm so glad you asked that." Alas, none of the questions submitted from the Swiss office were selected this time around. Nevertheless, their disappointment did not dampen their enthusiasm, and when Mr. Alfred thanked them all for attending, the room erupted in unison, and in a multitude of accents, "Thank *you*, Mr. Alfred!" followed by applause.

And so, as the employees of the Swiss affiliate of the Calculated Risk Group filed back to their respective offices, many slowed to observe the door that was next to the entrance to the conference room. It was the door to the apartment the company kept for use by its CEO, Mr. Alfred; the insurance genius who calculated, correctly, that companies would willingly pay an extra fifteen percent premium on their premiums to the Calculated Risk Group for no particular reason. And the mere fact that they did so would convince other companies to do the same for fear of missing out on an advantage that did not exist. Yes, some employees even reverently ran their fingertips across the door's wood, as if it were a religious relic; as though touching it might cause some of Mr. Alfred's genius to rub off; to enter their souls through an immaculate osmosis. Although Mr. Alfred had not used the apartment during the living memory of anyone now working at the Swiss office, the employees filing past it were filled with a quiet joy, which accompanied the certainty that he would one day, in the flesh, return to them.

The Underwriters of the Property & Casualty department went back to the second floor and again began typing on their keyboards with an even greater, almost messianic intensity, all privately anticipating unusually large bonuses this year. Urs Gipfeli had been absorbed in a calculation for the renewal of a policy for the Italian bank, *Credito Fumigazione,* one of Calculated Risk's biggest accounts. There was casualty insurance and travel insurance for 453 of the bank's top executives; property insurance for its 240 offices worldwide, including its fleet of corporate jets; various other sub-insurance policies for certain employees, and of course, cyber insurance, which *everyone* needed these days — all calculated to have them pay ten percent more in premiums than they did last year, topped off by Mr. Alfred's *premium* premium of fifteen percent. It had taken Urs weeks to complete it all while simultaneously working on his other accounts. As was his way, it was done consequently and methodically, and finished ahead of time, for it was Friday, and it did not have to be submitted to the client until ten o'clock on Monday morning. Ahead of time and without falling behind on any of his other work. Some days Urs Gipfeli worked himself to near exhaustion, hardly ever getting to spend time with his wife and young son, but he never questioned whether it was worthwhile. This was his reward: taking a minute to immerse himself in the immense sense of pride and accomplishment his completed work provided. He sat back in his task chair and savored the moment. Pure efficiency. As precise as a Swiss watch or a drill performed by the Swiss Reserve Army, of which he was an *Oberleutnant*, he reminded himself. This is why companies paid the extra fifteen percent premium on their premiums that Calculated Risk always built into their bottom line. They were reliable. And not just reliable, but reliable and steady as a . . . as a . . . *but wait*. What is this? As Urs Gipfeli perused his computer screen, the feeling of satisfaction and pride at a job well done suddenly turned to befuddlement. He noticed something he had overlooked. A subfolder containing a smaller piece to the *Credito Fumigazione* account. The bank had a policy on perishable food;

various cheeses and sausages as well as Chianti that *Credito Fumigazione* shipped once a week to its executive dining rooms all over the world. There was also a separate policy for a huge end-of-year Christmas shipment of braciole that the bank sent, not only to all its full-time employees, but also to its 'preferred' clients all over Europe, to the Americas, and as far afield as Hong Kong, Wuhan, China, and elsewhere in Asia. All this required Urs Gipfeli to calculate the premiums on insurance policies from thirty-eight points of production spread out all across Italy to Leonardo da Vinci airport in Rome, then to cities around the world, and from those destination airports to their final destination offices. He was suddenly stuck. Overwhelmed. He had never seen this piece of the policy before. He never even knew it existed! How does one even begin? How does one even start to calculate the loss ratio for all the pecorino or sobrasada that might spoil or just disappear in transit? Not to mention all the wine bottles that could leak or be smashed. He needed more information, a *lot* more information, before he could even make a dent in it all, and he needed it now. Who else had worked on this account? He saw from the file that it was Gustav Held. He looked up from his keyboard at Held's vacant desk and urgently tossed out the question, "Where is Held?"

The typing on keyboards ceased simultaneously as blank faces looked up over their computer monitors. "He was here this morning," Jason Peel noted.

"Was he?" Malvina Panchevska asked inquisitively, looking directly at Jason who immediately went flush. "I don't remember seeing him."

"I saw him upa stairs at the conferenza," Agostina said with certainty.

"He watched Mr. Alfred and just went home?" Urs Gipfeli said. "What kind of person would do such a thing?"

"He no go home. He musta be in the batharoom."

Hana duVal walked leisurely into the office, over to Malvina, and gave her a friendly neck massage. That had become fairly common; the two had gotten to be friends outside the office and attended yoga classes together once a week. Jason felt his crotch swell as he watched Malvina grin, and sensually roll her eyes up in her head in response to Hana's hands kneading her neck and shoulders. Jason had often fantasized about doing that to Malvina himself, but knew that if he ever tried, he'd be hauled down to H.R. immediately and possibly fired.

How unfair, he thought. He noticed Hana smiling at him as he watched. Again feeling himself blush, he looked away and over at Agostina who was staring longingly at Hana as she worked Malvina's neck. Noticing Jason's eyes on her, Agostina put her hand on her own neck with a come-hither look, which terrified and repulsed Jason, causing him to lock his gaze intently on his computer screen and type frantically.

"Where's Held?!" Urs cried out, now almost in a panic.

"He's working from home today," Hana said casually, as she went to her own desk.

"He's not online!" Urs shouted, pointing at part of his computer screen where the Microsoft *Teams* surveillance software monitored who was working and who wasn't. He quickly started typing Held a lengthy email listing all the information that he needed to complete the *Credito Fumigazione* account renewal. This was at six-thirty p.m. By the time he had finished his email to Held, it was nearly eight-thirty and the office was empty.

Jason Peel was the first to arrive Monday morning at 7:45 to find an exhausted, very disheveled and oily-looking Urs Gipfeli typing on his keyboard.

"You all right, mate?"

"Held never answered any of my fucking emails! I have left messages on his phone and he never called me back! I've slept for two nights in this *verfluchten Büro!* Things are impossible to find. Nothing is where it is supposed to be with this account. It is all *durcheinander!* I am an officer in the Swiss Reserve Army! I cannot work in this . . . this *chaos!* Whole files are missing! I cannot find any histories, there are no claims ratios, I don't even know what our exposure is! Now I've fallen behind with all my other work!" he shouted, storming out of the room just as Agostina was walking in with the cup of espresso from the cafeteria in the basement, almost knocking her down. "What is this with you people and your *huere-schiess-Braciole!'* he snarled at her angrily. "Is it your god? Do you pray to it?! *Where is Held?!"*

"È un pazzo," Agostina said, brushing splashed espresso from her bosom. "Whatsa wronga with him today?"

Jason shrugged. "I think he spent the weekend in the office."

Agostina went to her desk and put down the espresso. She took some photos out of her handbag, brought them to Jason, and set them on his desk while he stared at a spreadsheet on his computer screen. "You knowa who she is?"

Peel looked at each of the three small black-and-white photos of a shapely young woman on a beach in a bathing suit. "Is that . . . *you?*" he said, stunned.

"*Si*. Very beautiful, no?"

"Yes, very beautiful indeed." He had almost let the words, *what happened to you?* pass through his lips when Hana walked in and offered her usual, halfhearted, "Good morning" as she walked to her desk. A minute later, Malvina did the same. As she sat down, Jason seized the opportunity to make conversation by holding up Agostina's photos.

"What are those?" Malvina asked as she got up from her seat and went around to Jason's desk. "That is *you,* Agostina?"

"*Si*. Very beautiful, no? I was a *modella* years ago."

Hana also appeared at Jason's desk to take a look. "Oh, so beautiful," she said.

A rare moment of genuine, personal camaraderie was smashed when Urs Gipfeli burst through the glass doors and into the office. He startled everyone by shouting, "Where is Held?!"

So stunned was the group by Gipfeli's disheveled, raging appearance that no one spoke.

"I have a deadline! The *Credito Fumigazione* renewal! I've fallen *behind!* I could have been working from home all weekend. I could have spent ten minutes with my son before he went to bed. But instead of that I was here looking for files that don't exist! Held has them. Where is he?! *Where is Held?!*

"Credito Fumigazione?" Hana said, immediately knowing the importance of that account. "When is your deadline?"

"At ten o'clock!"

Hana ran to her desk, grabbed her cell phone and called Held. It went straight to voicemail. "This is Hana. We've got a huge problem with Credito Fumigazione. Call me back immediately!"

Urs panicked, "He will not call back! I've been trying to reach him since Friday night!" He pointed to his computer screen, "Look! It's eight-ten and he is not even online! He has not been online all weekend. He is not working at all!"

Hana instructed everyone to drop whatever they were working on and help Urs with the Credito Fumigazione account. The importance of the renewal to the company and their bonuses was so obvious that they immediately leapt into action. Frantically typing, they checked all the other accounts Held had been working on, looking for the misplaced files and spreadsheets, occasionally finding fragments of documents that might have pertained to the food insurance portion of the Credito Fumigazione policy, but in the end were useless. They tried accessing various other databases in the company for the information they needed, called employees in other departments, all while checking that portion of their computer screens every few minutes to see whether Held was online, always in vain. Finally, they had to face the hard reality. It was futile. It would have taken the team many hours of collaborative work on this account, and nothing else, to do all that was necessary to complete the renewal. And it was now a quarter to ten. Without comment from anyone, all activity ceased. The room seemed to deflate. It was an unconditional surrender. There was silence.

"Urs, see if they will give us an extension," Hana said, demoralized. "Until the end of the week. Tell them one of our people has been out sick."

With the room dead quiet, Urs Gipfeli typed out a couple of lines in an email to

Benito Ravanello, Credito Fumigazione's Chief Risk Manager, and clicked the SEND button. Within thirty seconds his phone rang. Urs answered, "Gipfeli," and was instantly hit with a barrage of verbal abuse from a very angry man so intense that he could not get a word in. "Signore Ravanello . . . Yes, but . . . Signore,—"

Ravanello was so agitated and shouting so loudly that the entire room heard him without being put on the speakerphone, "Now you tella me dis? I have a deadaline! I can no submit my budget ona time now! Calculateda Risk is makea me anda my teama look bad! Now we falla behind! And you takea twenty percenta more than anyone elsea!

"No, signore, there is a *fifteen* percent premium on our premiums."

"Basta!" And another verbal assault began.

Urs motioned for Agostina to take the phone and whispered, "See if you can talk some sense."

"Signore, questo è. . ." But she was hit by the same verbal barrage, and was not able to get a word in herself, only repeating, *"Si, si. . . Si. . . Si . . . Signore, Io pens . . . Si, si . . . Un momento . . . Un . . . Un momento."*

Agostina pushed the phone back at Gipfeli, "He wanna talka to you."

Urs took the phone and was lambasted again, this time slowly, menacingly, "You put a *lady* ona telephono? You calla yourself a man? *Bastardo!* Forka you, eh?!" Then Ravanello hung up.

The room knew the devastating implications of what had just happened. Everyone felt numb.

"Let's give him a couple of days," Hana said, finally. "Maybe he'll cool off. We should probably give Accident & Health a heads up. They might be affected here."

"Oh, that's just brilliant, Hana!" Jason shouted sarcastically. "Why not just ring Mr. Alfred directly and tell him we'd all like to forfeit our bonuses this year?"

The others voiced a similar frustration with that idea. Hana relented, "Okay, let's see what happens in a few days."

There was a ping from Hana's computer. An email had arrived. "Held has been written sick," she announced. "He won't be in for the rest of this week."

So, the underwriters in the Property & Casualty office at Calculated Risk, Switzerland, decided to give Signore Benito Ravanello, Chief Risk Manager at Credito Fumigazione in Rome, Italy, until Thursday to 'cool off.' On Thursday, Urs Gipfeli would again attempt to make contact with him. The group even discussed whether they should send some traditional *Landjäger* hard sausage as a peace offering, but came to the conclusion that Signore Ravanello would probably construe a gift of Swiss food as yet another insult.

But on Wednesday, news came that Signore Ravanello had moved Credito Fumigazione's entire business to the Diversified Risk Group, one of Calculated Risk's chief competitors. That meant not just the Property & Casualty business, but also its life insurance policies, accident and health insurance, as well as the insurance for Credito Fumigazione's corporate artwork. All of it. That Diversified Risk's employees had to have worked around the clock for days to nab the account was unspoken but obvious. They accepted the challenge and had managed to capitalize on the failings of Hana duVal's division. That brought recrimination from Calculated Risk's other departments down on the underwriters of the Property & Casualty unit. Winston Balls, manager of Accident & Health, was incensed, "What the bloody hell? You wankers have really bollocksed this up! Are you all a bunch of knobheads down there on the second floor?! Don't expect anyone else to take the blame on this. This is all your doing! It's coming out of your bonuses! And on top of it, when I go home tonight I've got to explain to my wife why we're not getting a braciole this year!"

Agostina was offended, "Why they get a braciole and noa us?!"

"Who cares about a *huere-schiess-Braciole!*" Urs shouted. "I need my bonus! This is all because of Held!"

"It is Held's fault!" shouted Malvina.

"Bloody Held," grumbled Jason.

"I cannot stand this man," Gipfeli said of Held. "It is Friday; he has not been online at all for the whole week! We have fallen behind!"

"Everyone has a right to be sick," Hana said with some sympathy. "We'll manage when he's back on Monday. We'll all just have to pull a bit more."

"I never been asick," Agostina said bitterly. "Not onea day since I worka here. Eight years!"

"Sick or not, I work!" Jason said. "If I have a raging fever and I'm coughing up a lung, I still sit in front of my computer at home, morning till night. I hold up my end."

"I don't trust Held," Gipfeli said. "I don't know why he was hired in the first place, not to mention as senior underwriter. It has always been a complete mystery to me. He is simply not qualified.

"Of course Held is qualified," Ana protested. "He has an extensive resume. And he has a PhD."

"Then why is he still an underwriter? Jason wondered. "Why hasn't he moved higher? Urs is right, I don't trust him, either. Something doesn't add up. He's nearly the same age as Mr. Alfred, for Christ sake!"

"I miss Tink LoHool," Malvina said whimsically, referring to the underwriter Held was hired to replace. "He knew what he was doing."

"He was manic," Jason said. "A bloody machine. He knew how to work, that bloke did. Days, nights, weekends, holidays, anniversaries, kid's birthdays, Christmas day, New Year's, in the office, at home; wherever the hell he was, he worked. We never fell behind while he was here. The bonuses always got bigger and bigger every year. If he wasn't sitting here, you could always see that he was online, never off. I used to see him online at two and three in the morning. You could reach him any time of the day or night. He worked, worked,

worked, right up to the day he had a heart attack."

"Has anyone been out to the Sanatorium to see him lately?" Hana asked.

"I went there once. He drooled on me," Malvina said with disgust.

Agostina shuttered, "Blah, adrooola."

"I have the greatest respect and love for that man," Urs Gipfeli declared. "He was my role model. No, more than that—my guru, my teacher. I would gladly spend many hours communing with him if they had not put him so far away. But it takes twenty minutes to go there with the car. Forty minutes with the S-Bahn!"

When Monday came, everyone, as usual, was in the office before eight o'clock in the morning. Only Held's chair was vacant. No one mentioned his absence until the clock struck eight-thirty precisely, when Urs Gipfeli stopped typing and suddenly sprung from his task chair.

"*Huere-schiess-Dräckchchch!* It is eight-thirty!" he shouted, throwing his arms up, no longer able to contain himself. "Where is Held?!"

Then, with the precision timing of an *Audemars Piguet Flying Tourbillion Chronograph*, an email arrived at Hana's computer. Held had been written sick for an additional week.

"I do not believe this!" Urs Gipfeli was beside himself. "Another *week?!*"

"Is he in hospital?" Malvina asked.

"He's faking it," Jason insisted. "Who is sick for two bloody weeks straight?"

"A doctor has written him sick," Hana said firmly, annoyed as much by the group's reaction as by Held's email.

"What kind of doctor?" Urs said sarcastically. "It must have been a psychiatrist. The man is obviously crazy."

"*Fottuto ragazzo,*" Agostina mumbled in disgust.

The group's continued remarks exasperated Hana who now was unsure whether she had been right to defend Held previously or not. She was uncharacteristically harsh when she shouted, "Can we just all get to work, please?! We've fallen behind. There's a lot to catch up on!"

And try to catch up they did. For the rest of the week the underwriters of Calculated Risk's Property & Casualty department toiled from early morning until nine or ten in the evening, going home only to work a few hours more. They calculated quotes; worked on new product development; there were the usual constant meetings with underwriters from other departments, or video conferences with other offices in Europe or America; all on top of the work of planning forecasts; checking compliance issues with the *Finma*; completing the renewals, for which they all now took extra care; following up with existing accounts; checking payments; all interspersed with those nagging, unpleasant, and nerve-racking peer reviews—the time-consuming video interviews with underwriters in other departments in which the quality of their quotes were checked, but did nothing to advance the Property & Casualty unit's own work—all of it the endless grind of the insurance world in Switzerland in general, and at Calculated Risk in particular. The successful completion of all of it was necessary to advance the careers of the underwriters; to forge ahead to positions of greater prestige and more money. All of it was being hindered by the absence of Held.

Yet the fact that Held was not in the office didn't stop any of his colleagues from throwing mountains of work at him via email, not simply in the hope that he would try to get something done while sick at home, but with the full expectation that he would strain to do all of it, no matter what it took. They labored under that assumption, not just because it was what any of them would do without question, but because the ramifications of him not doing so could be ruinous for Held's career. And in the canon of the Swiss insurance and banking theology, career was holy above all else.

On Friday morning, at about eleven, the sound of typing on keyboards was broken by a shout from Jason, which was a combination of disbelief and excitement: "Held is online!"

There was a sudden silence as everyone checked their screens. "He is opening his emails!" Malvina shouted. The room filled with the sound of furious typing as the group shoveled even more work at Held via the Internet, writing him emails with new projects in attachments, which also asked about the status of projects they had sent previously over the last two weeks.

At ten-thirty Friday night, the group dragged themselves out of the office, exhausted. They would all be working over the weekend from home, but carried with them a lightness from the knowledge that Held was back at work, and the certainty that they would be hearing from him over the weekend about the status of projects he had been sent. On Monday he would again be at his desk and working to exhaustion, just as they all had been doing since the Credito Fumigazione debacle, the ramifications of which they all still dreaded. Held was responsible for that, they all knew. Even Hana was done with him.

Urs Gipfeli, for one, could not wait to make Held's life a living hell. "Senior Underwriter, *mein Arsch*," he mumbled bitterly to himself in the tram on the way home. I am an *Offizier* in the Swiss Reserve Army, he thought. I know many ways to make men suffer!

On Monday morning, everyone drifted into the office early, each looking worn out by a lack of sleep. By 7:15 they were all at their desks—except Held. He had, however, responded to a handful of the dozens of emails each of the team had sent to him, but only with a few words in each asking for clarifications of their lengthy requests for information or quotes on accounts.

No one mentioned Held. No one talked about the weekend. There was nothing to be said about it. Everyone knew what everyone else did: work. They all had seen each other online from the early morning until late in the evening, Saturday and Sunday. That Monday morning, greetings were mere grunts that acknowledged each other. Hana,

Malvina, Jason, Agostina and Urs kept to themselves and buried their heads in work. Jason didn't even have the energy to drop a pen on the floor so he could quickly observe the shape of Malvina's legs crossed under the desk, which the slit in her long skirt, Jason's favorite, had amply exposed. Aside from the sound of fingers attacking keyboards, the room was silent. Puffy, bloodshot eyes stayed glued to computer monitors. Yet there was an underlying tension that came to the surface when Agostina, racing against a deadline and rubbing her aching wrist, gave some of that 'admin stuff' to Malvina saying, "I needa you to help with this." Malvina, buried under spreadsheets of her own, went ballistic, shouting "I'm not your slave! I'm not here to do your work!"

A loud shouting match followed, which was mediated by Hana with the result being that everyone got even more work piled on them.

It wasn't until eight o'clock, the group's usual start time, that Urs Gipfeli became visibly agitated, often turning toward the door as if he was expecting someone to arrive. He was able to control himself until eight-fifteen when he jumped up from his seat and shouted, "Okay, now he's just playing with us!" Everyone stopped what they were doing and looked at him, bewildered. *"Held!"* he shouted at them. "Where is he? I got sentence fragments in emails from him with questions to my questions. He did nothing all weekend. I did not see him online once. And again he is not here. Where is he?"

"Sit down, mate," Jason said as he began typing again. "When he comes he comes. Does no good to twist your knickers over it. We all have enough to deal with here without listening to you rant."

Held didn't come that day. Nor the next. He didn't show up at the office for the rest of the week. He was spotted online, though, working from home. Yes, actually working, answering many emails and submitting projects, though not nearly at the pace of the others. Yet it came as a relief that he was, at last, helping deal with the backlog that came from falling further and further behind.

At the end of the week, an announcement was made about bonuses for the Property & Casualty department. Lower than last year, and much lower than they had hoped for before the Credito Fumigazione disaster. It was the first time the group did not receive a bonus that was substantially more than the year before.

"It could have been worse," Hana said. "It's not great but not as bad as I feared it would be. At least we got something."

Urs Gipfeli thought he had finally found a way to make Held suffer. "Held should give up his bonus so we can split his share among ourselves. He was responsible for this."

Though it was in her power to deprive Held of his share, Hana was noncommittal, uttering only, "We'll see."

"Why do you want to reward him for his bad behavior?" Malvina asked angrily.

"Yes, that is a bad thing youa doing, Hana," Agostina said. "Helda did alota damage to us."

"He was written sick," Hana said. "He's been working again from home. He must have been quite ill."

"You cannot be serious, Hana!" Urs Gipfeli shouted. "He is making a fool of you!" Then he turned to Jason, who had been quiet through the entire conversation, and asked what he thought.

"I'll just be happy with whatever they give me," He answered lethargically.

Urs was so upset that he took refuge in the lunchroom in the basement. Winston

Balls, head of Accident & Health, walked past his table and sarcastically asked, "Blow up any accounts lately?"

"It was Held. He negotiated a contract on food that I knew nothing about. By the time I found out it was too late. How was I supposed to know that the Credito Fumigazione was flying cheese and sausages all over the world?"

"Woe to that man who comes between an Italian and his provolone," Balls said. "Held, eh? He's a bit of a strange duck. Where has he been? I used to see him down here every day crying into his cell phone."

"What do you mean, crying?"

"I'm not sure I should be telling you anything about all this. It's really none of my business."

"You can tell me. I'm an officer in the Swiss Reserve Army."

"Oh, I see. Well, in that case, every day I'd see Held down here pouring his insides out to someone about how he hates this job. How he never should have gotten into this business. How he hates everyone he works with. How he can't do the work because he's completely burnt out. He was bitter about the amount of work being dumped on him. He actually said he wished to be sacked."

"Held wants to get fired? How can that be?"

"I heard it myself. You know when people are emotional and they're talking into their cell phones and don't realize how loudly they're speaking? That was Held. Every afternoon. He talked constantly about different ways he might be able to retire early; if he contributed so much now to his retirement account, it would give him so much a month. He obsessed about the size of the capital sum of his retirement plan— my capital sum this, and my capital sum that. But it never worked out, no matter how he figured it. He was never able to calculate a sum he could live from if he retired early. I don't know why any human being would put up with listening to that from him day after day. There are all kinds in this world, I suppose."

"*Hmmmm*, Interesting. That explains a lot."

"Doesn't explain how you blew up Credito Fumigazione." Then Balls scoffed, "Ha! Swiss Reserve Army. You people have done nothing but sit on your arses polishing your boots for two-hundred years."

Back in the office, Gipfeli shared what he had just learned. "I just ran into Winston

Balls from A&H. He told me that Held hates this job and wants to be fired."

"And how would he know?" Jason asked.

"Because he heard Held talking on the phone."

"If Held doesn't want to work here he can just quit," Jason said. "No one is holding a gun to his head. Stop listening to rumors from people who have no respect for you."

"And what makes you think Winston Balls has no respect for me?"

Because no one respects you, Jason thought, but said, "Because that bloke has no respect for anyone but himself."

Monday morning, Urs Gipfeli made certain to be the first one in the office. When all the underwriters were present he made an announcement. "I have done a little research over the weekend," he said proudly. Everyone looked up at him. "Hana, you said Held had a PhD. What subject is his doctorate in?"

"Actuarial science? Math? I'm not sure."

"Wrong! Held has a PhD in philosophy! . . . *In Philosophy!*" He turned his computer monitor around so everyone could see. "Held wrote this book. It's called *Rhetorical Ethics*. I don't even know what that is supposed to mean. They let you look inside the book on this site. There is a parable about a communist and a Nazi who stab each other in the buttocks during a brawl in a beerhall. None of it made sense to me. And it is six-hundred and thirty-four pages long! He likes to spend hours musing over things no one in their right mind cares about! He is not an insurance man! He does not see the value in calculating premiums on risk. He thinks spreadsheets and cross-selling are unworthy of his brilliant mind. He has no appreciation for the importance of what we do here!"

"Why are you so obsessed with Held?" Jason asked. "Okay, he bollocksed up our bonuses. I don't think he did it intentionally. And you were working on the Fumigazione account, too. We could just as easily blame you as him. You need to relax, mate."

"Relax?! *Relax?!* I believe in this company. I believe in the fifteen-percent premium on our premiums, even if no one knows why companies are willing to pay for such a thing for no reason. As far as I am concerned, that is what makes Mr. Alfred a genius. It is why I believe in him, too. I cannot sit by and watch Held make a mockery of everything I love!"

"I don't care whether Held wrote a book or not," Hana said. "I've decided that he's not entitled to a bonus this year. We will split his share. I'll send an email around with the details."

"Be sure to copy Held in," demanded Gipfeli.

"Of course he will be copied in," Hana said. "He is still a member of this team. He deserves to be told that he is not getting a bonus in an email rather than to his face."

The day after Hana copied everyone in the department about the bonus split, she received an email from Held saying he had been written sick again, this time for two weeks.

"This is insane!" Urs Gipfeli shouted when he learned Held was sick again. "Why don't you just fire him, Hana? He is making a fool of us all."

"He can't be fired as long as a doctor has written him sick. You know that, Urs."

One night, days later, Urs Gipfeli again ran into Winston Balls, this time on the Paradeplatz waiting for the tram on the way home.

"I hear you people have fallen far behind," Balls told Gipfeli with some satisfaction.

"It is Held's fault. He keeps being written sick."

"Sick? I saw Held having dinner and drinking a beer at the Zeughauskeller last night after work."

"And he was not sick?"

"Pink-cheeked and healthy as ever. From the way he was attacking those sausages and potato salad, his appetite was quite ravenous."

"You are sure it was Held?"

"Yes, indeed. He raised his beer glass to me."

"I knew it. He's not sick! He's doing it intentionally!"

"Now Property & Casualty are a man short, eh? That's bad. You'll never catch up, I'm afraid. But you should expect that from Held. The man wants out."

"If it were up to me I would have kicked him to the gutter a long time ago. He never should have been hired in the first place."

"Well, now you know why he keeps getting sacked."

"Sacked? From where?"

"From where? From everywhere. I know people who have worked with Held at Acceptable Risk, Remunerated Risk, Denominated Risk, Mitigated Risk—he's been sacked from all of them. Or, as you Swiss so non-confrontationally like to put it, he was *invited to pursue other challenges*."

"Fired from all? Why does a man like that keep getting rehired? How is that possible?"

"Why wouldn't anyone hire him? He's been axed from an impressive list of companies. The *crème de la crème*. And he's got a PhD. You're looking at this backward."

A tram pulled up to the platform. "Are you getting on this one, Gipfeli?"

"Yes, of course."

"In that case I'll wait for the next. Goodbye."

For Hana duVal, being the manager of a department that lost a major account in a brutal meritocracy like Switzerland's banking and insurance sector could have but one inevitable result: she was promoted. In a couple of months' time, Hana was to become the new Head of Digital Sales Product Development. Her ideas for selling cyberbullying insurance to parents of young children had impressed the higher ups enough to kick her upstairs. In the natural progression of things, her successor as the Property & Casualty Manager, Switzerland, would go to the senior underwriter: Held.

"This means we will be working for Held?" Malvina asked, astounded. "We have all been working here much longer than he has."

"That can noa be. I will nota worka for that man."

"This cannot stand, Hana!" Urs shouted. "How are we to work under a man who has a disdain for all that we do?"

Hana was somewhat offended. She saw the rebellion as questioning her authority. "No decision has been made. There is nothing to get upset about. And maybe some congratulations would be nice."

"Congratulations, indeed, Hana," Jason said as he typed, staring into his computer screen.

"Thank you, Jason. Now let's everybody get back to work. We're swamped. I don't know how we're going to work through all of it."

And swamped they were, even as new work kept pouring in from other places: The Paris office had been asking for the renewal conditions for a slew of companies, for the reinsurance structure for several accounts for the coming year, as well as the forecasts for premiums, and details on premium growth for various clients. They also wanted calculations for loss ratios by line of business, and the lapsation rate for some critical accounts. The P&C underwriters were as far behind on all of that as they were on their own work. Then the office in London was insisting that the group get on with the peer reviews, which they had not even started yet. "Switzerland P&C have not done any of their peer reviews," London complained to Paris in an email, which all the departments in the Zürich office were copied in. "Yes, they should be ashamed," was Paris' REPLY TO ALL response.

Hana duVal's Property & Casualty unit was under siege from all sides; from departments within the Zürich office, as well as from Calculated Risk's offices elsewhere in Europe. The work kept pouring in. They had fallen hopelessly, and catastrophically behind. DuVal and her team were worn out, working in the office, well into the night from home, and every weekend. They all looked depleted physically, their tempers were short and all were suffering various stages of carpal tunnel syndrome from typing. They could all be seen at one time or another taking sudden breaks to massage their wrists or simply stand and stretch. And they were never able to get even with, much less ahead of the work. It was worse than any worst-case scenario. Even Mr. Alfred's mantra, *"When you think you can't possibly work any harder, push yourself even more. That's when miracles happen,"* wasn't inspiring them. There was nothing miraculous in any of this; there was only hopeless drudgery.

In the men's room, a voice in the next stall asked, "Is that you Gipfeli?"

"Yes, it is me."

"I thought so. You are the only one who wears army boots with a business suit."

"I am an offic—"

"Yes, yes, I know; Swiss Reserve Army and all that"

"To whom am I speaking?"

"Balls, here. Your man Held is still sick, is he?"

"Don't get me started on Held. He is a disgrace to this organization. His actions are killing us in P&C."

"I only ask because I've been seeing him almost every day at lunchtime."

"You have seen Held? Where?"

"His favorite place seems to be the James Joyce. I've had a series of lunch meetings there with brokers in the last week. I saw him between noon and one o'clock each time. Say, could you slip me some toilet roll under here? . . . I'm afraid I'll need more than that, I'm British! . . . Look, why don't

you just take a bit for yourself and give me
the rest."

The thought of Held eating lunch at the
James Joyce Irish pub, just a few minutes'
walk from the office, where he could easily
be spotted, made Urs Gipfeli fume, especially
with the group's workload now insurmountable
because of him. Gipfeli had never liked Held.
He had never thought him up to the job. He
had even heard that the company insisted
on giving Held a bigger salary than he had
initially asked for when they hired him:
140,000 francs a year instead of 130,000.
Germans in Switzerland were always willing
to work for less, undercutting the salaries of
Swiss nationals. Those fucking Germans, Urs
Gipfeli thought; always pushing themselves
into the affairs others. At least Malvina, the
Pole, Agostina the Italian, Jason the Brit,
and even the American Hana, all knew in
their hearts that Switzerland offered them a
better life than they could ever hope for at
home. They accepted that fact with a quiet
acquiescence. But the Germans were all so
bossy. They relished the confrontations that
the Swiss tried so hard to avoid. They thought
their *Schriftdütsch* German was *so* superior
to the Swiss *Mundart,* even when theirs was
the language of the Nazi concentration

camps and ours was as innocent and cozy as a family sipping *Alpenbitter* around a fireplace in a snowbound chalet. Urs had graduated from the prestigious *HSG* —The Hochschule St. Galen, Switzerland's elite business university. It was the place where the nation's future leaders gained practical, useful knowledge. Held had a PhD from one of Germany's diploma factories, where every useless thought had to be analyzed and turned over and discussed and rationalized endlessly for years and years. Now the self-proclaimed philosopher king was mocking them all by drawing that 140,000-franc salary every month without even working for it. And they were not allowed to fire him because he found a *huere-dütscher* doctor who was willing to keep writing him sick! Held was gaming the system. Urs Gipfeli made it his mission to get him; to expose the invader and repel him from the company, if not from the homeland itself. It was his sacred, sworn duty as a member of the Swiss Reserve Army.

Confronting Held at home, even if Gipfeli knew where he lived, would do no good. If he was sick he would be expected to be at home. Urs would have to get him at a place he should not be if he were really sick—like lunching in the middle of town.

Every afternoon for days, between noon and one o'clock, Urs Gipfeli ordered an expensive hamburger at the James Joyce, waiting for Held to arrive. But Held never entered the place. He stayed longer than one o'clock, arrived earlier than noon, cutting into his work time, and still—no Held. Finally, he asked a waiter if he had seen a man with sandy-blond-graying hair, about such and such a height and weight; a description so broad it could have been any of five men in the place, none of whom were Held. Gipfeli then took out his cell phone and went to the Calculated Risk company website where Held's photo was shown with the other P&C underwriters.

"Ah, yes, I do know him," the waiter said in his Irish brogue. "That's the man who hates his job."

"He told you that?"

"Constantly. Every time I brought his food, or refilled his glass, he would tell me how awful his feckin' job was. How much he disliked the people he worked with. He said he couldn't even bring himself to look at the work anymore. He would go on and on about how much he wanted to retire early, running through different schemes about how he might swing it financially; you know, writing various calculations in a small notebook. He talked *ad nauseam* about something called a feckin' capital sum in his retirement plan; how it wasn't big enough. No matter how he figured it, he fell short every time. Sometimes it seemed he would be on the verge of cracking it, then I would go back to his table and it was just no good. He just could not find a way where he would have enough money to meet all his obligations without earning. He said he needed to earn even more than he already was."

"He told you all of this? He talked about his capital sum?"

"He did, yes. I listened because he was a good tipper and I felt terrible for him. It was clear that the man was suffering. He made me very glad I'm a waiter and not an insurance man. And I *hate* being a feckin' waiter.

"So where is he now? I've been in here every day spending thirty-five francs on a stinking hamburger and a handful of *huere-schiess-Fritte* and have not seen him!"

"How the hell would I know where he is? What's it to you, anyway?"

"I work with him. So where the hell is he? Where is Held?!"

The waiter looked down at Gipfeli and noticed his army boots. He grimaced in disgust. "So you must be the feckin' idiot who is shouting his head off all the time. He told me about you. You should learn to modulate your voice. You get on everyone's feckin' nerves."

Hana duVal had grown increasingly angry with the amount of time Urs Gipfeli had spent away from his desk at lunchtime. One hour and fifteen minutes had become two hours, and by Friday, it was just over three. All while the group was exhausted, hurting physically, struggling with fatigue and short tempers, while, nevertheless, falling exponentially further and further behind on their workload. None of the other underwriters in the Property & Casualty unit were leaving their desks over the course of the long eight o'clock in the morning to ten o'clock in the evening workday. Lunch and snacks were brought from home. An empty seat signaled a quick trip to the men's or ladies' rooms. Nerves were frayed all around. Hana, while ready to leave this mess behind and start her new position, had to see it through until a new head of department was named. And she was very concerned that not getting a handle on the workload might jeopardize her promotion. So when Gipfeli finally reappeared in the office after his latest sojourn to the James Joyce to try and track down Held, she could not help but unload on him.

"Urs, where the dickens have you been?" she cried out. "We're buried here!"

Her tone was so unusually harsh that the entire room went silent. No one had ever heard Hana shout that way before.

"I've been trying to track down Held! I've been told that he was eating lunch at the James Joyce every day. I spoke to a waiter who had seen him there!"

"Are you kidding me? Held? Get into your seat and get to work!"

"Hana, you do not understand! The company is paying him as well as adding to his capital sum, even though he has stopped working. That cannot be allowed to continue!"

"If it's any consolation, Calculated Risk is not paying Held's salary now. We are insured for employees who are written sick for extended periods. Elliptical Risk is paying. So just get to work! You've done enough damage here.

"You cannot talk to me that way, Hana! I am an officer in—"

"Will you please just get to work!"

Everyone began typing feverously. A few minutes later there was a shout from Malvina, "Held is online!" Everyone shoveled projects at him with a vengeance via email, not just in spite-lust, but also the genuine hope that he would help them dig out from the hole they were in. Those emails went unopened.

It did not take long for Hana to feel ashamed of the way she had lashed out at Gipfeli in front of the others. Yes, his obsession with Held was damaging to her department, but she, too, had had it with him. She realized how lucky she was to have been kicked upstairs and not out of the company all together, and attributed it to the hard work of her colleagues over the years, including, and probably especially, to Urs Gipfeli. He was the closest thing to Tink LoHool in his prime. So to try and make amends, she decided to mail each of her coworkers a small gift: A copy of the book, *Real Leaders Bathe Last* by Burgess Boomsier, the number-one bestselling author in the *management self-help* genre that had just been released in Switzerland. Everyone would be happy to have it, Hana thought. And with the exception of Jason Peel, all of them were. Urs Gipfeli spent the night inhaling it, even after a long day and several hours working from home. Malvina Panchevska sent Hana a text message thanking her, saying how she looked forward to reading it, and how much she missed their coffee dates away from the office. Agostina took it very much to heart, thinking that it was sent to her in preparation for being named Hana's successor, filling her with an excitement that made it impossible for her to sleep. Her eight years working herself ragged were about to pay off, she thought. Jason merely flipped through the pages before throwing it on a table, thinking that it is only Americans who are impressed by such rubbish.

Yes, Jason Peel had been undergoing a personal crisis of self-doubt ever since Calculated Risk lost the Credito Fumigazione account. Or more precisely, when he was reminded of the man he had worked next to for five years: Tink LoHool. Since the day Malvina mentioned LoHool's name, Jason could not get him out of his mind. LoHool had dedicated his life to the company. He was always there for his colleagues, no matter what they needed or when. Yet, when he was gone he was all but forgotten, recalled only when they were nostalgic for a workhorse, and even then, ridiculed as a man who drooled. Jason realized that LoHool was the only person he had known in his years in Switzerland who had ever done him a good turn. There was that day when Tink LoHool gave Jason Peel a new pair of shoelaces. "Thought you might be able to use these," LoHool said, as he tossed the tightly-folded, stiff brown laces bound in a paper wrapper on Peel's desk. At the time, Jason was perplexed. Why did he think he needed them more than anyone else he knew? He wondered whether LoHool had purposely bought them in a shop, or did he just find them somewhere—in a drawer at home, perhaps? Yet, thinking about it now touched him. Now it was much more than just a mystery. Jason found himself longing for more of Tink's Flemish camaraderie in the office. We could certainly use some of that these days, he thought.

Agostina got to work before 7:30 in the morning the day after receiving *Real Leaders Bathe Last* with the expectation that Hana would surely want to speak with her privately about being named manager. But when Agostina entered the office, Urs and Hana were already huddled together at Hana's desk. "I think the entire department has to be organized along military lines," Urs said. "That is always the most efficient; Burgess Boomsier is quite right about that, I believe."

"Yes, I thought that was an interesting section of the book, too," Hana said. "I think he is onto something there."

"You know that I am an officer in the–"

"Yes, yes, Urs, I know all about that by now."

"So, we agree, I am the man to take over the department."

Agostina could not contain herself when she overheard that last line, "Hey, what's agoin' on here!"

"I will be taking Hana's place when she moves into her new position," Urs said proudly.

"Urs, I did not agree to that. Nothing has been decided, Agostina."

"I worka here longa before you, Urs!"

"It has nothing to do with how long we worked here," Urs said. "It has to do with ability."

"*Capacità?* Ha! Becausa you loosea the Credito Fumigazione account! Signore Ravanello tella me that you are the biggest Swissa assahole he know!"

"I did not lose the Fumigazione account! That was Held!"

"I rather worka for Held thana for you!"

Amid the shouting, Malvina entered the office, "Whoa, what is happening here?!"

"Urs think he gonna be the new head of the departamento, even though he loses Fumigazione!"

"I did not lose that account!"

"What?!" Malvina shouted. "How can Urs just be appointed without any discussion?"

"Everyone just calm down!" Hana shouted. "No decision has been made yet. Stop this bickering! We've got work to do!"

And to work they all went, but the tension and resentment in the office was, and remained, palpable. Agostina secretly felt so hurt and embarrassed at having misconstrued the meaning of Hana's gift that she felt as though she might breakdown and cry. No one mentioned Jason Peel's absence that morning, though Hana had tried to reach him by phone a couple of times since nine o'clock. It was almost 11:30 before Jason walked into the office.

"Jason, where were you?" Hana asked, trying not to let her annoyance show, but failing. She felt that she was losing control of the group.

"I went to the Sanatorium to visit with Tink LoHool," he said, taking his seat at his computer.

The office went quiet.

"You should have called to let me know you were going to be late. I left two messages with you."

"I didn't notice. And from the looks of the place it doesn't seem I missed anything."

"You miss a lot! Urs think he'sa going to be our new boss." When she said that, Agostina again was so overcome with a sense of shame at having misinterpreted Hana's gift, and anger at the certainty that she was going to be passed over in favor of Urs, that she stood up and hurried out of the office to the ladies' room. She spent a few minutes there composing herself, then went down to the lunchroom in the basement. As she sat there feeling sorry for herself and pondering her life, Winston Balls approached.

"*Buongiorno, signorina!*" he said cheerfully. "Don't normally see you down here taking a break . . . May I?" he asked, pointing to the empty chair at her table. Agostina nodded. "You're looking rather unhappy. Everything all right?"

"Everything ok. I justa missa my Milano."

"Yes, I can well imagine you do. Switzerland is a beautiful country, and it runs like the proverbial watch . . ." Balls looked to see whether there was anyone in the immediate vicinity, then said quietly, "But the Swiss *are* a bit dull, aren't they?"

Agostina smiled, "I guess you musta missa your Engaland too."

"As a matter of fact, I don't. Not one bit. Listen, I know things are somewhat chaotic in P&C right now. I've heard you've fallen hopelessly behind since the Credito Fumigazione disaster. Luckily we up in Accident & Health have had a gangbuster year, so it really didn't affect us much."

"Everything'sa fuck up upa there. Held is always sicka. Now they wanna make Urs Gipfeli the new head of the departament."

"Gipfeli? *Really?* The man in the army boots?"

Agostina laughed, "Yes, you believea that?"

"But you've been there much longer. Why aren't you the next in line?"

Agostina felt as though she might cry and looked down at her lap. "I know. And I worka harder than anyone elsea there. Malvina and Urs doa nothing. Peela too."

"Agostina, how would you like to come and work for me?"

"In A&H?"

"Yes, as senior underwriter. Baron von Käsekopf is returning to the Fatherland, and I really don't feel like interviewing a parade of thirty-something know-it-alls in skinny suits."

"Siegfried is quitting?"

"Yes, he is. And if he weren't I'd have sacked him. He's gotten awfully grumpy lately; just can't take the pressure anymore. And I would like someone with your experience who would pick up the job right away. No falling behind."

"I feela bad leaving Hana."

"Hana? She's already left you. She is moving on, remember? And you just said Gipfeli is taking her place. Come work with me. I will increase your salary by ten-thousand francs. The bonuses will be bigger every year. Sleep on it and let me know tomorrow. I'll work it out with Hana." Balls confidently rapped his knuckles on the table and stood up, "*Ciao, bella!*"

Meanwhile, up on the second floor, the group were discussing Jason's visit to the Sanatorium:

"How is LoHool?" Malvina asked.

"I don't think he knew who I was. He sat right there for years working his arse off," Jason said as he motioned to Held's empty desk, "and I don't think he remembers this room or anyone in it. No wonder Held wants out."

"If Tink LoHool heard what you just said he would be ashamed of you!" Urs shouted. "He dedicated his life to this company."

"Yeah, and look at where it got him. Why don't you go visit your *guru* and try asking him if he regrets working here."

Gipfeli nearly jumped out of his seat, "*Blaspheme!*"

"Jesus, Urs, calm down. Bloody hell."

"I am tired of people in this company who don't appreciate the importance of our work!"

Jason laughed, "You sound like Mr. Alfred. I'm finally beginning to understand Held. I don't know why he ever came back here after what happened to him with the François Thiéry account."

"Mr. Alfred is a genius!" Gipfeli cried out.

"So now you are feeling sorry for Held?" Malvina said, defensively. "*Really?*"

"Stop this bickering!" Hana shouted again, throwing a file down on her desk like a school teacher.

Agostina returned to the office and was immediately admonished by Hana, "You can't just disappear like that! Where have you been?"

She didn't answer, but at that moment made the decision that she would take Winston Balls' offer, and sent him an email saying so.

The next morning, as soon as Agostina entered the office, she was approached by Hana, "I got a call from Winston Balls last night. You can't leave now, Agostina. We are already hopelessly behind and shorthanded."

"That's a no fair! Where is Held? He'sa no even here. He noa work at all for weeksa and still getting paid. He'sa why we falla behind."

"Regardless, we all have to pull really hard right now. I can't afford to let you go."

The next morning, Hana got an email saying that Agostina was written sick for the rest of the week.

"This is insane!" Urs screamed. "How is her work supposed to get done? Agostina is copying Held! She isn't even online!"

"She would never do that to us," Hana said, taking her cell phone and dialing Agostina's number. It went straight to voicemail, "Agostina, I have to know what you are doing. You can't leave us in the lurch like this! Please, call me back!"

"She is doing what Held is doing. He has poisoned everything!" Malvina shouted.

Jason sat at his keyboard typing with a grin on his face.

"Why are you sitting there with a dumb smiling?" Malvina asked, making a rare mistake in her normally perfect English. She was obviously riled.

"I'm just sitting here doing my job," Jason said.

"No, you are not," Urs said suspiciously. "You have changed. You are one of them now, aren't you? A subversive. You're here to gum up the works."

"I'm just sitting here doing my job," Jason reiterated, grinning.

"Will everyone please just stop this bickering and get to work!" Hana shouted.

A couple of hours later, Urs' telephone rang. He answered, "Gipfeli."

There was a lot of background noise; people at a restaurant. "Is that you Gipfeli?"

"Yes! This is Urs Gipfeli!"

"Winston Balls here. Listen, I just finished up a lunch meeting at the James Joyce and I happened to see that your man Held is here, too. Thought you'd like to know."

Urs cupped the phone with his hand. "Held?" he whispered. "He is there now? Are you sure?"

"I'm looking right at him across the room. He's eating a hamburger and chips in a big booth all to himself. Ah . . . he just waved at me. I'm waving at him now. Anyway, I'm off; heading back to the office. Goodbye."

Urs Gipfeli's mind went into overdrive as he struggled mightily with what his next course of action should be. His impulse was to go and confront Held. Urs had dreamt of finding him at the James Joyce and snapping a photo of him eating lunch when he was written sick. He might be able to get Held fired if he delivered that damning intelligence to H.R. But doing so would require him to abandon his post. He looked around the room: Malvina, Jason, Hana, all staring at computer screens with bloodshot eyes and sour looks on their faces while typing. Held's seat was empty and now Agostina's was as well. They were absent without leave, and suffering no consequences whatsoever. Urs looked over at Hana. Deep down he never had respected her. She wasn't competent to lead. She had let Held off too easily for too long. He was responsible for all this mess. His decadence set off a cascading sequence of events that had destroyed the cohesiveness of this unit. What was his game? Who could have put him up to it? Gipfeli was determined to find out. He had to confront Held. He could not ignore the call of duty. He went over the route in his head, calculating how long his mission might take. He knew it was a seven-minute walk to the James Joyce from the office. He could make it in three. Five minutes or less to confront and photograph Held. Three minutes back. It wouldn't take him longer than a trip to the men's room.

Urs stood up, stretched his arms over his head, mumbled the words, "bathroom break," and walked out of the office, leaving his coat behind. When he was out of sight of his coworkers he bolted to the street. Timing himself with the chronograph on his wrist, he made for the Pelikanstrasse, reaching the restaurant just within the projected time, though he was much more winded than he had anticipated. No matter, he thought. The mission must continue according to plan. He barged in, scanning the long room for Held.

"He's gone," someone said. It was the waiter Gipfeli had spoken to previously.

Gipfeli was panting so hard he bent forward and put hand on his knees, "What?"

"I assume you're after the man who hates his feckin' job."

"Held. Where is he?" Gipfeli asked, straightening up and taking a deep breath through his nostrils.

"I just told ya, he's gone. You missed him by ten minutes. He had a good day, though. Said he finally figured out how to grow his feckin' capital sum by enough in the next twelve months to be able to retire early. God, I feckin' admire that man. You, on the other hand, look like something feckin' awful. You should get some sleep."

Urs was so distraught that he didn't bother hurrying back to work. He limped along at his normal pace, shivering in the cold, with the big toe of his right foot developing a blister in his army boot.

Back in the office Gipfeli passed the small, glass-walled conference room where Hana was speaking to another woman he had never seen before.

"Who is that woman speaking with Hana in the conference room?" he asked the group as he took his seat. No one knew.

But it did not take long to find out, for five minutes later the two women walked into the office.

"Urs, you are finally back," Hana remarked with an annoyed expression before addressing the group. "Okay, everyone, I need your complete attention. Please stop what you are doing. This is Fawn Diller from our office in Hartford. She's been sent to us to evaluate how things are working around here."

Fawn Diller took a step forward and spoke with hands clasped in front of her, "I'm so happy to be here in this beautiful city, this beautiful country, and to meet all of you." She asked Hana, "Is this the whole group?"

"Two of our colleagues are out sick, I'm afraid."

"Oh. Well, it is certainly nice to be here and to finally get to see our affiliate here in Zürich. Since it is my first time here why don't we begin by having each of you introduce yourselves and tell me a little about yourself. Everyone has a story; everyone's story is important. Why don't we start here." She pointed at Malvina.

"My name is Malvina Panchevska. I come originally from Warszaw—"

"Oh my goodness!" Fawn interrupted. "And where on earth is that?"

Malvina raised an eyebrow and cautiously said, "It is the capital city of Poland."

Jason looked at his lap and snickered. Fawn Diller was plainly embarrassed. Hana stepped in, "Jason, why don't you introduce yourself."

"I'm Jason Peel, Englishman. Been labouring here as an underwriter for six years, three months and twelve days."

Fawn waited for Jason to elaborate, but when it was clear that nothing more was coming, she moved on:

"Urs Gipfeli. Underwriter, also for six years. Officer of the Swiss Reserve Army. Disciple of Mr. Alfred."

The expression on Fawn's face was confused; not sure what to make of what she had just heard. There were a few moments of awkward silence before she said, "Well, thank you all for that. Very interesting group we have here. Okay, so it is only fair to let you all know that some changes are coming. We are just in the preliminary planning stages. But you will all be kept informed along the way."

There was an email ping from Hana's computer. She walked over and read it. "Oh," she said with a smile, "it looks like Held will be back with us on the fifteenth."

"Held?" Fawn asked.

"Our senior underwriter. He's been out with health issues."

"Well, that is excellent news," Fawn said. "I'm looking forward to meeting him." Urs Gipfeli grimaced and turned red-faced. Hana's piercing stare told him to keep quiet. "It was very nice meeting all of you,' Fawn said. "I'll be seeing you again very soon."

"I'll walk you out," Hana said.

"A disciple of Mr. Alfred," Jason mumbled derisively under his breath.

"Something is coming," Malvina said as she eyed Hana and Fawn walking down the hallway. "I don't have a good feeling."

Urs shook his head in disbelief, "Hana is just going to let Held come back? How can that be after everything he has done to us?"

"I bet he will be taking over the department after all," Malvina said. "We have to do something against that. Jason, don't you agree?"

"I really don't care at this point."

"How can you say that?!" Gipfeli shouted. "Held destroyed our bonuses. He ruined our whole year! He made all of us look bad. He is the reason the changes are coming. How can you let him just get away with that?"

"Urs is right, Jason," Malvina said. "And Hana doesn't care. She is leaving soon, anyway. It doesn't matter to her."

"Look," Jason said lethargically as he typed on his keyboard and stared into his computer screen, "they are going to do whatever the bloody hell they please. There is nothing we can say about it."

"You are *wrong!* We can forge a united front! We can keep Held from breaking through!"

"Urs, stop shouting," Malvina said. "You are always shouting."

Before the end of the next week, the group was told that Fawn Diller wanted to meet with each member of the team individually, one-on-one, including Agostina, who was now back in the office. Either because of guilt or because her whole identity was hopelessly tied to her work, her strike lasted only three days. She was, nevertheless, still very angry and unhappy.

Jason Peel was the first to be called into the conference room where Fawn Diller was waiting.

"So, Jason, nice to see you again. I know you are all very busy, so this won't take long. Tell me, how did you wind up in Switzerland from the UK?"

"The same reason everyone winds up here: high salaries and low taxes. I make twice as much here as I did in the UK. Then there is the beautiful scenery. The Alps. Fresh air. That's about it."

"Uh, that's interesting. So how is everything going in Property & Casualty?"

"Everything's fine. Had a bit of a problem at renewal season, but those things happen."

"I understand it affected the bonuses this year. Doesn't that upset you? I mean, you said you came here for the money."

"I did. But I guess it isn't so important anymore."

"The money isn't important?!" Fawn was clearly stunned by Jason's statement.

"There was a man who worked here for many years. He dedicated his life to this company. I visited him at a Sanatorium the other day. He exists in a state worse than death. Kind of puts things in their proper perspective. There are things more important than money and career, right? Wouldn't you agree?"

Fawn was stunned, "Well, uh, yes, of course. I'm just, uh, well, interested in everyone's story. Everyone's story is important—"

Jason, staring at Fawn inquisitively, interrupted, "Do you read Burgess Boomsier books?"

Fawn, caught off guard, took a few moments to answer, "Yes, as a matter of fact I do. I find him instructive and insightful."

"I thought so. I have a mountain of work to catch up on. Is there anything else you need to know?"

Fawn suddenly felt as though she had been uncovered as a secret, foolish celebrity groupie. The 'story telling' technique was a Boomsier method for breaking the ice with employees; for getting them to trust their bosses by making management seem to care about the people who work for them.

Nevertheless, she forced herself to push on. Clearing her throat, she asked, "How would you describe your coworkers? Everything working out?"

"Everyone works very hard; late nights, weekends. We are under tremendous pressure at the moment. Everyone does their best. That's about all there is to say about it."

Jason stood up, "Nice chatting with you." Obviously the session was over, and not in the way Fawn had anticipated. She was confused, as much by Jason's candidness and lack of striver's drive, as by the feeling that she had somehow failed Burgess Boomsier. Strangely, Fawn felt deeply embarrassed by her admission that she read his books. She did not meet with any of the others that afternoon. Fawn Diller went to a pub instead.

When Peel arrived back at his desk, Urs, Malvina and Agostina immediately wanted to know about the interview. Jason just slid back in his seat, started typing, and contemptuously mumbled, "Utter tosh."

Yet the next day, Fawn Diller was again in the office, determined to continue with the next round of 'story telling.' She began with Agostina.

"So nice to meet you, Agostina. You were out when I first met the others."

"Yes, I was a sick lasta time." Agostina seemed reluctant to answer any of Fawn's questions at first, but her hesitance soon gave way to a firehose of grievance.

"You wanna knowa my story? I worka here longer thana anyone elsea! I doa everything! Thisa place geta nothing done without me. Gipelfi loosa the Credito Fumigazione! We getta almost noa bonus thisa year! I shoulda be the senior underwriter. Insteada they hire Held! I should be the nexta in the line for head of departamenta! You know Winstona Ballsa froma Accident & Healtha?"

"*Win. . . ?* Oh, yes, I know Mr. Balls."

"He know how good I am. He wanna me to worka with him. Even fora more money! Hana won't leta me go, even whena she's gonna goa too! It's noa fair! I am trapped like a slavea here!" Then she stood up and left the room, violently slamming the door behind her in anger and shaking Fawn so much that she had to take refuge in the ladies' room to collect herself.

When she returned to the conference room, Malvina was already there waiting for her. "Hana sent me in," she said, sitting there with legs and arms crossed.

"It's all Held's fault," she said, even before Fawn had a chance to sit down.

"What do you mean, Malvina?"

"You want to know stories? That's the story. It's all about Held. He is out sick constantly. He is never online. I get work thrown at me from every direction; working all hours of the day and night. It's all Held's fault."

"You are the first to tell me this."

"It's Held. He is the reason you are here."

Fawn was genuinely confused, "I'm sorry, I don't understand what you mean."

"I know what is going on. It's all about Held. That's all you need to know." Then

Malvina got up and left the room, leaving Fawn bewildered.

But even more bizarre was her meeting with Urs Gipfeli. "I know he is not sick," he said about Held as soon as he sat down. "I am an officer in the Swiss Reserve Army. I have my Intelligence sources. Held is a fifth column playing us all for useful idiots."

"But Hana told me that he's been written sick by a doctor."

Urs gave a whoop of laughter. "Held found some *huere-dütscher* doctor to keep writing him sick. You know how those Germans are; they stick together. You cannot trust any of them. They are always scheming to take over everything. If he was so sick that he cannot even open his emails, then how would he be eating lunch every day at the James Joyce bar?"

"Have you seen him there?"

"*No!*" Urs shouted, banging his clenched fist on the table, making Fawn jump. "He has eluded me every time! But I know he was there. Like I said, I have my sources. You don't know about him. Held hates his job. He wants to be fired. He is really not an insurance man at all. He is a *philosopher!* The kind of man who thinks useless thoughts, then writes them down in a jumble of words no one can understand.

He's not a normal human being like we are. He doesn't believe in Mr. Alfred like we do. Find out what he is up to. Find out who he is really working for. Most importantly, find out how he plans to grow his capital sum in the next twelve months! That is the story behind everything. Let me know what you uncover."

"I'll . . . I'll do my best," Fawn said, completely disoriented and nervous at being alone in the room with Gipfeli. She tried several times to politely wrap up the interview but Urs wasn't having it.

"You know he was only here for a short time, yet he was hired as the senior underwriter. And why? That is another thing that needs to be investigated, wouldn't you say?"

"Well, thank you very much for this information, Mr. Gipfeli. I think I have enough—"

"You know that Held was fired from multiple insurance companies and was hired here despite that? That is very suspicious, I think. Wouldn't you agree?"

"Why, yes, that is very interesting, thank you again for—"

And so it went, with Fawn Diller trying to end the conversation while Urs Gipfeli showed an unhealthy and unhinged obsession with Held.

While Urs Gipfeli was making Fawn Diller feel increasingly uneasy in the conference room down the hall, Hana entered the office after a trip to the ladies' room, walked to Malvina, briefly massaged her neck, then returned to her desk. The massage was a mechanical imitation of what it once was, but nevertheless, for Malvina a welcome interlude that had become a rarity over the tense past few weeks. Jason, busy with spreadsheets, did not take notice. Malvina had become aware that Jason no longer paid attention to her. He no longer took those nonchalant glances at her; no long dropped things on the floor when she wore certain clothing. He didn't seem to care when men from other departments dropped by to make small talk or ask her to lunch, even though those visits had become rare because everyone knew Property & Casualty had fallen so catastrophically behind that people from other departments did not want to be seen associating with them unless absolutely necessary. In any case, the tension in the Property & Casualty office had become so palpable, that any casual visitor felt unwelcome. So detached did Jason seem that Malvina felt she could no longer get him to take some of her workload with a simple smile or hand on his shoulder the way she used to. Jason's disinterested lethargy bordered on contempt and had come at the time when Malvina felt she would need him as an ally to navigate whatever big changes were about to happen. Hana could not wait to start her new position and leave this mess behind. All the late nights trying to catch up on work meant the two had not bonded at yoga class in weeks; Malvina felt she could no longer depend on her for protection. Agostina had always disliked Malvina, considering her a cheap flirt, and she, too, was eager to leave the department. Malvina had always been able to manipulate Urs as easily as she had Jason, but Urs was acting stranger and more bizarre by the day. Malvina felt she needed Jason, yet Jason had drifted away. So Malvina Panchevska kicked off her right shoe and slowly ran her foot up Jason Peel's leg to his knee and then into his thigh.

Jason, staring at his spreadsheets and sensing something out of the ordinary, stopped typing. Then he pushed himself away from his desk, jumped out of his seat and shouted, *"Bloody hell!"*

Everyone stopped what they were doing. "What's happened?!" Hana shouted.

"She's rubbin' her foot on my crotch!"

Hana and Agostina were staring at Malvina, wide-eyed and slacked-mouthed.

"*Piccola puttana,*" Agostina mumbled.

"No, no!" Malvina shouted in a panic, "I was just stretching my leg! I have been sitting much too long!"

"I'm reporting this to H.R.!" Jason yelled.

"Stop, stop, stop!" Hana stood up from her seat. "Everyone just calm down. Jason, I'm sure she didn't' mean to—"

"Then why is her bloody shoe off! I'm reporting this to H.R.!"

Malvina was on the verge of tears, "Jason, please, I didn't . . . "

But he was already out the door.

Just as Jason exited the office, Urs Gipfeli entered, straight from his interview with Fawn Diller, "She is on the case!" he announced. "Diller will find out the secret about Held's capital sum! I am sure she will inform Mr. Alfred personally about what is going on here! Now it will all come out! We will soon know what Held is up to!"

He was ignored as Hana went to Malvina and asked what the hell had happened. "It is a misunderstanding," she sobbed into her hands. Agostina sat behind her computer observing it all, thinking the department was becoming a madhouse.

"Did you not hear me?!" Urs shouted. "Fawn Diller is beginning an extensive investigation into Held!"

"Urs, please, enough with that!" Hana barked, as she took Malvina, sobbing, out of the room.

"You gotta serious problema, Urs," Agostina said, shaking her head as she began typing. "You maka yourself and everybody elsea crazy."

As a result of Jason Peel filing a sexual harassment claim against Malvina Panchevska, each of the underwriters in the Property and Casualty department was required to be interviewed about the incident with H.R. In the end she was reprimanded but not fired. The embarrassing story did, however, spread quickly throughout the Swiss office and beyond, making Malvina the subject of lewd jokes, sharp glances, and not very concealed laughter between coworkers from other departments when they saw her in the hallways. As a result, she never left the P&C office while in the building. She neither looked at nor conversed with the other underwriters in the department unless absolutely necessary, and even then in such a weak voice it was difficult to understand her. She became a monotonous shadow who sat in front of a computer and worked. Jason was feeling so detached from everything involving the office and the people working in it that he never felt guilty about reporting Malvina. He, like everyone else, sat before his computer joylessly working, day after day, at the office, at home, and on the weekends, never able to make a meaningful dent in the workload. They had long ago reached the tipping point; the dreaded place, that until now was more folklore than reality, where they had fallen so far behind that they could never hope to catch up. And the entire company knew it. The group seemed to exist in a black hole that was slowly sucking the life out of them. Yet, even in that state, news that a major announcement was due within days created a sense of excitement; perhaps reassignments, new hires, or other changes that were on the way would alter the course of the group's endless purgatory of drudgery.

When the day finally came, Fawn Diller stood in front of everyone in the P&C department and introduced Winston Balls, "A man you all surely know by now." There was tepid applause.

"Thank you, thank you. I'm here to inform all of you of some big changes in the structure of the Property & Casualty unit here at Calculated Risk. It seems that H.R. has determined, based on your performance this year, that there is no one currently suited in this department to take on the role of leading it. Therefore, to make a long story short, it will be rolled into Accident & Health, which I lead, as you all know."

A general mumble of shock and disbelief filled the room.

"So thata mean we all worka for you now, Winston?" Agostina asked.

"Not exactly, Agostina. It means that you've all been sacked. It has been determined that it is most efficient to have my group, as overworked as we are, work a little harder. We are all anticipating miracles. You, unfortunately, will all be made redundant; or *invited to pursue other challenges*, as they say."

"That's a noa fair! Winston, I was supposed to worka for you!"

"Yes, well I'm afraid that's not possible now, Agostina. Sorry about that. The higher ups want to slimdown. But all of you, look on the bright side: you've all just been fired from the leading insurance company in the world. With that on your CVs you'll have no trouble finding work elsewhere . . . Oh, and Mr. Alfred is very proud of each and every one of you, *eh*, I'm sure."

"Mr. Alfred cannot know about this," Urs said. "Mr. Alfred would never approve of this. He knows how valuable I am to this organization. I am an officer in the Swiss Reserve Army. Only I am fit to lead this unit! This is all Held's fault! He has subverted everything! I demand you call Mr. Alfred right now and tell him about this subterfuge. He will not let this happen! I have dedicated my life to his work!"

"I'm afraid this was all Mr. Alfred's idea. Sorry, old chap. You'll find something else."

"No! I do not believe you! Mr. Alfred would never do this!"

"I'm afraid he has. Shareholder value and all that. You understand. Now, all of you will finish out the week, then collect your things. Everyone will receive the standard three months' sev—*Gipfeli, what the devil are you doing?!*"

There was a collective gasp as everyone watched Urs Gipfeli climb out the window and move onto the ledge.

"I do not want to find something else!" he shouted, arms outstretched at his sides. "I believe in Mr. Alfred! I believe in the fifteen percent premium on our premiums! I will not work for anyone else! I will not settle for less!"

Winston Balls stuck his head out the window, "Gipfeli, have you gone mad? Get in from there right now!"

Hana pulled Balls out of the way, "Urs, come back in! Let's talk about it. We all love you here!" She looked back at the room for support, "We all love you, *don't we?!*" But no one uttered a word.

"Where is Held?" Urs asked in seeming desperation. "Today is the fifteenth. He was supposed to be back today."

Just then, there was a ping on Hana's computer. Agostina, standing near Hana's desk, clicked on it and read the email. "Held is a written sicka for two more weeks."

Upon hearing that, Urs Gipfeli, standing there on the ledge, began to weep.

Jason went to the window, "Urs, think of your wife and son. Don't do this to them. Com'on, mate," he said, reaching out his hand. "Come back inside. Let's grab a pint and talk things over."

"Where?"

"What?"

"Where will we drink a pint?"

"Uh . . . Where ever you like. We can walk over to the James Joyce."

With that, Urs Gipfeli let out an awful, hopeless groan, rolled his eyes up into his head, and leapt from the second-floor ledge of the Calculated Risk Group's Swiss headquarters.

A pleasantly cool morning breeze blew gently off Lake Zürich. Two men sat beside one another in wheelchairs on the green lawn of the Klinkhoffer Sanatorium, bundled in their bathrobes and blankets, observing the view.

". . . That was 2018," one of the men said to the other. "They thought I had given them a deal, but what they did not know was—"

The story was interrupted when a young female attendant dressed in tight white jeans and a white polo shirt brought them each a glass of orange juice. "*Grüezi, Herr Gipfeli,*" she said, adjusting the height of the tray on the side of his wheelchair and inserting a straw into the glass. Gipfeli, whose hands were bound in a straightjacket, leaned over and took a sip, though his neck brace made it difficult. The young attendant then did the same for Tink LoHool, who, with his head tipped awkwardly to one side, acknowledged with a grunt.

A doctor appeared and checked the vital signs of both men. "A couple of more days, Herr Gipfeli, and we will be removing the casts from both your legs," he said.

"Has it been eight weeks already?"

"Indeed it has. But don't expect to be walking anytime soon. Your legs were shattered. You will need a good deal of physical therapy. I doubt that you will ever walk unaided again."

"And what about this?" Urs asked, struggling with his arms.

"That will take somewhat longer, I'm afraid. After all, you did attempt to harm yourself by jumping out of a window."

"Herr Gipfeli," the attendant said, "there is someone here to see you this morning. He is waiting up in the main building. Shall I send him down, Doctor Bindl?"

The doctor nodded his permission before taking his leave.

"A visitor? I wonder who it can be?" Gipfeli said to Tink LoHool, who groaned while staring, unblinking, at the lake.

Gipfeli had to squint hard; the bright sun made it difficult to recognize the figure standing in front of him. "*Peel?*" he asked, genuinely surprised.

"Hullo, mate. When I found out that they put you here, I wondered whether you two would find each other. Tink, good to see you again."

"So, what is the news from the front?" Urs asked in so serious a tone that Jason was unsure whether he was delusional as well as physically broken.

"It's all gone, mate. Property & Casualty have been taken over by Winston Balls. He runs it all. Everyone in our department was sacked. Even Hana. Balls took her digital product ideas for insuring cyberbullying and tucked them into Accident & Health. They said it would be easier to market that way."

"Balls," Gipfeli muttered, whether in admiration or contempt was unclear. "And *Held?* Please tell me he's gone, too."

"No, they couldn't fire Held because he kept being written sick. He may not have gotten a bonus, but he wound up walking away with more money than anyone in the department. And he didn't even have to work for it. He's turned out to be the smartest of all."

"No! No, he was not smart! Held was a traitor! All of you people . . . You were not insurance men like Tink and me. Not one of you ever had what it took. We were the warriors for Mr. Alfred. We have the broken bodies to prove it!"

Jason didn't know how to react to that lunacy, other than to pity both of them. He sat down on the lawn next to Gipfeli. The three men observed the view in silence for a while: the white sail boats anchored in the lake, and the rolling hills beyond the shore, dotted with perfectly-manicured chalets.

Jason finally worked up the nerve to ask the question he had come to ask: if either of them had any regrets.

"None!" Urs answered without hesitation. "One does not regret his greatest love!" LoHool, trapped in his unresponsive body, gave a very loud and agonized shriek, that could have meant yes or no. No one would ever know whether he had regrets or not.

Jason didn't pursue it. He found the sight of both men so tragically sad that he went to Tink LoHool and gently wiped the drool from his mouth with the collar of his bathrobe.

"So where did you end up?" Gipfeli finally asked. "Are you with Delineated? Acceptable? Elliptical? Just don't tell me you are with Diversified; I hate those guys."

"I'm not working for any of them. I'm in training to become a tram driver."

"You are going to drive a tram?" Gipfeli laughed. "Are you joking?"

"Know what, Urs? I realized that the best part of my day was watching the city float by during my commute on the tram. So why not do it all the time, and get paid for it? I won't be stuck behind a computer all day; I'll get to ring the bell and wave at kids.

When I go home the job stays at the tram depot. Sounds bloody good to me. Anyway, I should go. Just wanted to stop by to see how the two of you were getting on."

"Peel!" Gipfeli shouted as Jason turned to leave. "Come by again sometime. My wife and son, they don't visit very often. I need to see faces from the good old days. Tink, he isn't very talkative."

Jason put his hand on Gipfeli's shoulder, "Don't worry, mate. I'll be back." The irony in 'the good old days' almost made Peel cry.

Days later, the two men were out staring at the lake in the morning, glasses of orange juice at their side, and having their vital signs monitored by Doctor Bindl.

"You will need several more surgeries, Herr Gipfeli," Dr. Bindl said while examining his cast-free, swollen and badly scarred legs. "The x-rays showed the pins in your right femur and tibia are not holding the way they should."

The female attendant came down from the main house.

"Fräulein Styrmark, why don't you prepare a warm bath for Herr Gipfeli," Bindl said, winking at Urs."

"Right away, Doctor. Oh, Dr. Held would like to meet with you in his office this afternoon at two o'clock, if your schedule permits."

"Tell him I will be there."

Urs' face became electrified, "Held? *Held?* Held is here? Where? Where is he? *Where is Held?!*" Gipfeli, increasingly agitated, began fighting to free himself from his straightjacket, "You do not know. . . You do not understand. He is not a real doctor. He is a *philos*—" Struggling more violently with the ties that bound his arms, Gipfeli shouted, *"Where is he?! Where is Held?!"*

Dr. Bindl urgently waved at two men, both dressed in white suits, who were sitting outside the main building. They ran into the house. A minute later they both came running down the lawn, one holding a syringe in the air. Urs was pulled out of his wheelchair and lifted over the shoulder of one of the two men while the other pulled down his pajama. Bindl injected Gipfeli in the buttocks. Within thirty seconds, Urs entered a state of exhausted calm.

"*Where is Held?*" he pleaded to Bindl one last time.

"Try to relax, Herr Gipfeli. Fräulein Styrmark, see that he gets an *extra special* bath."

The next morning, Gipfeli and LoHool were again pondering the view of the lake. Urs, however, was still agitated; his mind seemed stuck in the skipping grove of a vinyl record. He could not stop himself from barking the question, *"Where is Held?"* at Fräulein Styrmark, or at LoHool, or Dr. Bindl, or at the hills beyond the lake while feebly struggling to free his arms from the straightjacket.

Dr. Bindl decided that no additional sedatives should be administered just yet. "Let's keep an eye on him for now," he advised.

Tink LoHool was wheeled away for a therapy session, leaving Gipfeli alone, ritually muttering, "Where is Held?" as if it were a spell that would conjure him.

"Here I am."

Urs thought he must be experiencing a drug-induced hallucination. Held was standing right beside of him.

"Why is it? . . . How is it possible?" he said, astounded.

"I'm the new director of medical ethics," Held said happily. "You see, the salary I earn here is just big enough so that I can contribute enough to my capital sum every month to retire in one year . . . " Held took a small notebook out of the pocket of his white lab jacket; the pages were filled with one carefully written mathematical equation after another, each one crossed out. "Look, all of these failed, but I finally solved it. You see if I—"

"I don't care!" Gipfeli shouted, turning away. "Held, why did you abandon your post? Why didn't you open your emails when I needed your help with the Credito Fumigazione account? You are a disgrace to insurance men everywhere. You have betrayed Mr. Alfred!"

He fully expected to turn back toward Held to find that he had vanished; proof that the situation was a hallucination. Yet Held was still there.

"*I* betrayed? *Me?* Remember the François Thiéry account? I worked myself to the bone on that. I put in months, on top of all my other work, never falling behind. Do you know what it took to save that account? To bring it to profitability after Hana and the rest of you mismanaged it for years? All the legal work, all the negotiations over premiums, the translations, getting all of it through the *Finma*; all of that along with Mr. Alfred's fifteen percent premium? And what happened? All of you decided to kill it, because saving it made me look good and all of you look bad. After that I just could not do it anymore. I didn't know what the term 'burnout' really meant until I just could not do it anymore. Credito Fumigazione? You know the hours and hours of work it took to figure out the premiums on all that mozzarella and scungilli? Weeks and weeks— just that one silly account, *plus* all the other work. You people were throwing more and more of it at me constantly. And whenever I needed your help, whenever I asked you a question, I never got an answer. All you said was, *'What do you think the answer is?'* or *'Don't you know that by now?'* Blah, it all made me so sick to my stomach that I wanted to puke all over everything. Looking at those emails made me physically ill, which is why I had to get written sick. And every time I was scheduled to go back to work I felt sicker still. So I got written sick again. And when I was again supposed to go back I got even sicker, so, well, you get the idea."

"You weren't so sick to your stomach that you could not eat lunch every day at the James Joyce," Gipfeli said with a heap of sarcasm and disgust. "I know about that from Winston Balls!"

"Why shouldn't I have eaten there? I happen to like the James Joyce. The food is excellent. It was only when I looked at emails or thought about work that I felt like I was going to die."

"Then you should never have gotten into this business in the first place. Why did you? Why didn't you take your PhD and start spewing your philosophizing at students in some university from the beginning?"

"I got into it because it was what was expected of me. I've been working on my PhD in my spare time and between jobs for years. I completed it just before I started that miserable job at Calculated Risk."

"So why didn't you just quit, Held?! That would have been the honorable thing to do."

"I did. But only when I was ready. And let's not talk about honor in business. There isn't any. If there were, Calculated Risk would not be charging a fifteen percent premium on its premiums for no reason, and all of you would not have killed the François Thiéry account because it made me look good. In business there are only sharks like Mr. Alfred and Winston Balls. Why do you think Balls told you where I was eating lunch? It was only to try and foment trouble so that he might take some advantage. You people are all so predictable. That's why I was so focused on this," Held again pulled the notebook out of his pocket, put it in front of Gipfeli and began to explain his capital sum contributions, "You see the *percentage* had to be—"

"Nonsense! I don't care about your capital sum! The premium on premiums is what makes Mr. Alfred a business genius!"

"Or it makes him a con man. Either way, it doesn't make him an honorable man. After all, Mr. Alfred isn't here for you now, is he? He doesn't care what state you and poor LoHool were driven to. For him it's all and always about the *DOLLars.* I'm sure Mr. Alfred never bothered to ask how Tink is getting on. He was just another employee who fell by the wayside in far-off Switzerland who was supposed to sit there generating x-amount of revenues every quarter. When he could no longer do that, they just tossed him aside, hired me, and never gave Tink or his family another thought. There was no honor in it, Gipfeli. Not in Mr. Alfred, not in the shareholder value, not in the premium on premiums, not in the striver culture, and not in the way employees are expected to work until they drop . . . Or until they wind up in straightjackets. I'm sorry to have to say that, but it is true."

That assertion obviously made Gipfeli deeply uncomfortable. He sat there for a while with an expression of contempt on his face, then asked, "What exactly is it that you do here, Held? You write more of your incomprehensible gibberish that confuses people, like in your book? Stories about people stabbing each other in the buttocks. That is why you gave up a career with a company that holds our very civilization together?"

"Don't tell me you've actually read my book!"

"I looked at excerpts. That was enough."

"The moral of that knife-fight story is in the way the powerful advance their own interests by turning ordinary people against one another. Seriously, Urs, you were never a man of ambiguity; I won't discuss my work with you. Let's just say that, for the first time in my life, I enjoy what I'm doing. I found a way to stick it to Calculated Risk by getting written sick constantly. I made them pay me a lot of money while I did nothing for it, and they couldn't fire me—"

"You are wrong about that!" Gipfeli interrupted, as if he'd found a way to turn the table on Held. "We were insured against people like you. Elliptical Risk was paying your salary!"

Held shrugged it off. "Oh, well. That doesn't matter. I worked for Elliptical. They were Calculated Risk but with a better lunchroom."

To hear Held compare another insurance company to Mr. Alfred's Calculated Risk angered Gipfeli, "I'm sure you were fired from Elliptical just like you were from everywhere else you ever worked."

"I prefer the term, *invited to pursue other challenges*. And as a matter of fact, I was. Everywhere except Calculated. But even if they had been able to fire me I wouldn't have cared. By then I knew I had nothing to lose but my chains. Being written sick gave me time to think, Urs. You cannot think when your mind is cluttered with garbage constantly. In one year, I'll have the capital sum I need to retire early. But I don't want to retire. I like it here. After twenty-eight years feeding that monstrous machine, I found my soul. And to your point, if insurance really did hold civilization together, you and Tink would not be sitting here every day. What happened to the two of you was not civilized. It would not be tolerated in any ethical culture. You were driven by greedy people who used you to make themselves wealthy. Mr. Alfred said that if we pushed ourselves beyond the brink, miracles would happen. Well, the only miracle, Urs, is that you survived. I wish I could say as much for poor Tink LoHool.

Gipfeli went quiet. He seemed on the verge of tears when he muttered, "I loved that company." Held thought Urs might actually be harboring feelings of remorse.

"I know you did. But your love went unrequited. No, Mr. Alfred isn't here for you. People like him are just leeches feeding off the rest of us. But guess who is here for you? I am. Held is here! So try to forget about all that now. Concentrate on putting your life back together. Instead of chasing bonuses and thinking of new ways to swindle people, why not find something to do with yourself that you will be proud of when you look back on it. Try to be happy. Nobody in that business was happy." He waited for a response, but Gipfeli just sat there grimacing. Again, Held wondered whether he was reconsidering his priorities or experiencing feelings of regret, which would have signaled a breakthrough in the healing process that his psychoanalyst should be informed about. "We can talk about all of that later, Urs. You are going to be here a while. Come, let's go back inside." Held took hold of Gipfeli's wheelchair and pushed him toward the main building. "You know, tonight is Italian night at dinner. They are serving braciole."

"*Huere-schiess-Braciole*," Gipfeli mumbled bitterly.

Where is Held?

Alternative ending
Urs Gipfeli did not survive the leap.

Jason went to the window, "Urs, think of your wife and son. Don't do this to them. Com'on, mate," he said, reaching out his hand. "Come back inside. Let's grab a pint and talk things over."

"Where?"

"What?"

"Where will we drink a pint?"

"Uh . . . Where ever you like. We can walk over to the James Joyce."

With that, Urs Gipfeli let out an awful, hopeless groan, rolled his eyes up into his head, and leapt from the second-floor ledge of the Calculated Risk Group's Swiss headquarters.

The memorial service for Urs Gipfeli took place two weeks later. Hana duVal, Agostina Paffutto, Jason Peel and Malvina Penchevska all attended. Afterward, they decided it fitting to have a drink to their former coworker at the James Joyce pub since *James Joyce* were the last two words Urs Gipfeli heard on this earth. Jason Peel admitted the guilt he felt for uttering the name "James Joyce" and wondered whether

Gipfeli would still walk among the living if only he had suggested they grab a pint somewhere else. But how was he to know the feelings of hopelessness and futility that the name of the bar conjured in Urs? There was no way any of them could know, and that's what they all told Jason, and what Jason told himself. So they raised their schnapps glasses in a midafternoon toast as Peel said solemnly, "Here's to you, Urs."

Winston Balls, having concluded a lunch meeting at the James Joyce, passed the table on the way out with a business associate and noticed his former coworkers. He sent the associate ahead and stopped. "Well, you're all looking very glum. It can't be as bad as all that."

"Today was the memorial service for Urs Gipfeli," Malvina said, coldly.

"Oh, was that today? Sorry to have missed it. Tell me, was he buried in his army boots?"

"Not funny, Balls," Jason said without looking at him.

"Didn't mean to be snarky. It's just that it would have been a fitting tribute. You know, Swiss Reserve Army and all that."

"Urs was cremated," Hana said.

Truth be told, none of his coworkers ever liked Urs Gipfeli while he was alive, but they much preferred him to the man now hovering over their table, unwanted. As a matter of fact, each of them had, in their own strange way, come to believe that Urs Gipfeli had sacrificed himself for them; that he had died for their sins. All of them had made the decision to move on: Hana duVal back to America, Malvina Panchevska back to Poland, and Agostina Paffutto to her beloved Milano. They all wanted to find a new line of work. Only Jason Peel had decided to stay on in Switzerland, a country he genuinely liked. He would soon start training to become a tram driver. In his soul searching over the last months he had come to realize that his favorite part of the day was watching the city float by during his commute to and from the office on the tram. So now he had decided to make it his profession. One that stayed at the Tram depot when he went home in the evening, leaving him time to develop the social life he sorely lacked. So when Winston Balls mentioned that there was an opening for an additional underwriter in his overworked department, he was surprised when none of the group were interested. "We're out," Hana told him. "You'll have to make your miracles happen without us."

"Well, that's a shame," Balls said. "Agostina, really not interested? Not even for a hundred-forty-thousand francs a year? You know the bonuses will be big with me."

"Noa way, Winston. Not even for a milliona francs a year."

Winston Balls was left speechless. Suddenly, Malvina's eyes grew wide and she shouted in astonishment, "Held is here!"

Everyone looked to the back of the room, but didn't see anyone resembling Gustav Held. "Where?" asked Hana.

"There!" Malvina shouted, pointing at the television on the wall behind the bar. And there, sure enough, was a photo of Gustav Held over the shoulder of the anchor of CNNMoney Switzerland; the photo from the Calculated Risk website with his uneasy smile and vaguely disheveled look.

Simultaneous shouts of "Turn it up!" and "Make it louder!" startled the waiter behind the bar; the same Irish waiter who had interacted with both Held and Gipfeli.

"Why, that's the man who hates his feckin' job!" he said, pointing the remote at the TV and turning up the volume loud enough for all to hear:

"And finally, The Naked Risk Group announced today that Dr. Gustav Held will be its new European Director for Reinsurance

Underwriting. In a press release, Mr. Furby Loomis, NRG's regional president for Europe said, 'Dr. Held brings a wealth of experience and depth of knowledge gained over nearly three decades working for some of the biggest names in the insurance industry. We are very much looking forward to working with him as we continue to drive growth in revenue and earnings in this crucial market.' CNNMoney attempted to reach Dr. Held for his reaction and plans for his new role, but he was feeling under the weather and, unfortunately, unable to join us."

Everyone was dumbfounded. Finally, the waiter said, "That's how he cracked it! That's how he's gonna be able to retire early! He got a bigger job so he could earn more and grow his feckin' capital sum faster! God, I feckin' *love* that man!"

Winston Balls recovered from his amazement. "Why, yes, that's it. European director . . . that's *three-hundred-thousand* a year if it's a cent, excluding bonuses. He's feeling under the weather. Ha! I bet he gets to his goal without once stepping foot in their office."

"That man is my feckin' hero!" the waiter shouted, adding NRG's corporate slogan, *"A naked position is always at risk!"* and raising his hand for a *high-five* at Balls, who ignored

him but began to laugh uncontrollably. Big laughs from his gut bellowed through the place as he looked to the ceiling and shouted, "I told you, Gipfeli! You were looking at this backward!" He left the bar, laughing hysterically, and without saying 'goodbye' to the others.

"I don't begrudge him," Peel said of Held. "Not one bit. More power to him."

The group sat in silence for a while, then got up and went their separate ways, never to lay eyes on one another again.

Gustav Held entered early retirement seven months later, having been written sick by the same *huere-dütscher* doctor for the entire term of his employment at the Naked Risk Group.